Just Like Abigail!

MOIRA MILLER

Abigail is lovable and mischievous, and one thing's for sure – she's always in the middle of an adventure! Whether she's sailing a boat on the park pond, waving a rattle on the football field or making a new bedroom for herself in the attic, children will love to read about her.

These humorous stories about a thoroughly modern little girl are just right for reading aloud at bedtime or any time.

MOIRA MILLER

Just Like Abigail!

Illustrated by Doreen Caldwell

A Magnet Book

First published in Great Britain 1983
by Methuen Children's Books Ltd
Magnet paperback edition published 1984
by Methuen Children's Books Ltd
11, New Fetter Lane, London EC4P 4EE
Reprinted 1987
Text copyright © 1983 Moira Miller
Illustrations copyright © 1983 Doreen Caldwell
Printed in Great Britain
by Cox & Wyman Ltd, Reading

ISBN 0 416 47860 3

Contents

1 Abigail Goes to the Museum

'Mum,' wailed Abigail. 'I've lost my tooth!'

'I know,' said Mum. 'You told me yester-day. Remember?'

'I've lost it again,' said Abigail. 'I put it on the coffee table and it's not there now.'

'I see what you mean,' said Mum. 'It's probably underneath something. Have another look.'

Abigail shook out the old newspaper and looked under Dad's book and glasses case. There was no sign of the tooth.

'Well, go and ask your Dad,' said Mum. 'He had a tidying-up fit this morning. Maybe he's seen it.'

Dad was sorting through some packets of seeds in the garage.

'Mum says you're having a tidying-up fit,' said Abigail.

'Humph!' said Dad. 'I'm just trying to find a space in here to put things down.'

'I've lost my tooth,' said Abigail. She picked up a packet and peered inside at the tiny brown seeds.

'It's not there,' said Dad, taking the packet from her. 'And these grow lettuces not teeth!'

Abigail giggled. 'It was on the coffee table,' she said.

'Oh!' said Dad. 'You'd better have a rummage in the waste paper basket then. And put it in a safe place if you want to keep it.'

After tea he sat down to read the newspaper. Something small and white fell out of the case with his glasses.

'That's my tooth,' shouted Abigail. 'I put it in a safe place with your glasses.'

'Oh Abigail!' said Mum. 'Put it in the Tuppence Pot with all the other bits and bobs.'

'It's my BEST TOOTH!' said Abigail.

Dad put on his glasses and looked at the Best Tooth very carefully.

'It's a very good one,' he said.

'It's got real blood on it!' said Abigail, pointing to some little dark red marks.

'Magnificent!' said Dad. 'It really ought to be in a Museum.'

'What's that?' said Abigail. Dad looked at her over the top of his glasses.

'You don't know what a Museum is?' he said. 'Then we'd better go and visit one on Saturday. A Museum is a very useful place.

You learn something new every time you go there.' And that's all he would say.

'What's a Museum?' Abigail asked Mum.

'A place where they keep old things,' said Mum.

'Like the garage?' said Abigail.

'Well – not quite!' laughed Mum. Abigail asked Paul what a Museum was.

'A place where they keep Horrible Dinosaurs!' said Paul. 'We saw them when I went on the school trip.'

'Like a zoo?' said Abigail.

'No, silly,' said Paul, and that was all he would say. So Abigail had to wait until Saturday.

The Museum was a huge, high building of brown coloured stone.

'Fancy cleaning all those windows,' said Mum, as they walked up the stone steps.

'It's got a funny front door,' said Abigail. The big heavy glass door was like a roundabout; people stepped in and pushed it round.

'I'm going first,' shouted Paul, whirling round into the door. Mum went second.

'Now you go in,' said Dad, 'and I'll come last.'

Abigail stepped into a space in the door. It turned quite fast with a soft swishing sound. Suddenly she found herself back out on the steps again. There was no sign of Mum or Paul or even Dad.

'Ooooh!' she wailed. There was a banging on the window beside the door, and Mum and Paul were waving to her. Dad came out and took her hand.

'You're supposed to step out when you get inside,' he laughed. They went through the door together this time, into the Museum.

'Can I do that again? said Abigail, and before they could stop her she went back round the door three times very quickly.

'Can we have a door like that?' she said, tumbling out. She felt slightly dizzy and bumped into Paul, who pushed her back.

'Behave yourselves,' whispered Mum. 'They don't like nonsense in here!'

A tall man in a dark suit and shiny cap was standing watching them with a frown on his face. Dad took Abigail's hand and together they walked into a huge room with a cold black and white checked stone floor.

'Is this the Museum?' asked Abigail.

'Shh,' said Dad. 'Don't shout. This is just the first room, there's lots more.'

'It sounds funny,' whispered Abigail. There were people walking round the room, looking into glass cases and talking to each other quietly. Their voices sounded far away and very soft, and their feet clicked on the hard floor.

'It's because it's so big,' said Dad. He

stopped to look in a glass case. Abigail looked around her. The black and white squares made a pattern all over the floor. She slid both her feet on to a black square, then stretched out and stepped into the next black square without putting her feet on the white tiles. She stepped from there on to another black and then another.

'What are you doing?' asked Paul.

'Sharks'll get you!' whispered Abigail. 'You're standing on the white.'

'No they won't,' said Paul hopping on to a black square. 'They'll get him.' He pointed to the man in the black suit who was standing watching them. Abigail stepped into another black square and bumped into Mum.

'Careful!' said Mum. 'Come on, let's go and have a look round.' She took Abigail's hand and walked across the room to the door on the far side.

'Sharks'll get you,' whispered Paul.

'Aren't any, stupid,' Abigail hissed back at him.

They walked through smaller rooms full of glass cases. In some there were animals and Abigail stopped and stared at them. A huge stuffed hippopotamus with a sad face stared back.

'I'd like one like that,' said Abigail.

'You'd never get it into bed with Hot Dog,'

11

said Mum.

'Could use it for a table,' said Paul. 'It could stand beside the bed.'

'And where would you keep your clean socks and pyjamas?' said Mum. 'There's no drawers.'

'In his mouth!' said Abigail and everyone started to laugh.

'You lot are getting ridiculous,' said Dad. 'Come and look at something sensible.' He stopped at the door into the next room.

'Shh,' he said. 'Dinosaurs!'

Abigail stood behind him and peeped round. In the middle of the floor there was an enormous dark grey dinosaur, standing on a little wooden platform. His head almost touched the roof.

'Is it real?' whispered Abigail.

'No,' said Dad. 'That's just what people think they looked like. Nobody's ever seen a real one.'

'How do they know then?' she asked.

'They find teeth and bones and things,' said Dad. 'Come and look.'

Abigail looked in a glass case. A row of huge white teeth lay on the black cloth, smiling up at her.

'Bit bigger than yours!' said Dad.

'How did they come out? said Abigail. Some of the teeth were even bigger than her hands.

'Probably didn't brush them properly!' said Mum. 'Dinosaurs never did as they were told!'

They spent a long time in the dinosaur room looking at the teeth and bones. In one case there was a little jungle with two tiny dinosaurs having a fight.

'Look, you can see his insides coming out!' said Abigail.

'Yeeuck,' said Mum. 'Let's go and look at the pictures upstairs.'

They walked through huge rooms with shiny wooden floors. There were rows and rows of pictures in heavy golden frames. Abigail looked at pictures of flowers, pictures of people, and pictures of ships and animals.

'I'm tired,' she said. She stood on tiptoe and made her shoes squeak on the shiny polished floor. She walked right down the room on her toes. Squeak, squeak, squeak, squeak, past all the very grand people in the big pictures. They didn't seem to mind, but a tall lady with glasses turned and stared at her.

'Not much longer,' whispered Dad. Mum had stopped in front of a picture of a man with dark eyes and very black hair. Abigail stared at the picture and the man stared back at her. She pulled Mum's sleeve.

'Is that the man that looks after the Museum?' she asked. 'The one downstairs?'

'No,' giggled Mum. 'But it does look a bit

like him.' She walked on slowly looking at the other pictures. Abigail wandered out into the corridor.

Facing the door, and staring down at her was a tall statue of a lady. She was made of very cold white stone and had something that looked like a sheet wrapped round her. Abigail reached up and touched it. It looked soft, but the folds were cold and hard. She looked up the back of the statue. It was just the same, with the sheet hanging down in folds to her bare feet. Abigail touched one; they were big feet, with long straight toes. Tucked in between two of the toes was something bright and shiny. Abigail leaned over to see what it was.

'Hey, little girl, what are you doing?' The man in the dark suit and shiny hat was coming along the corridor. Abigail stepped back and stared at him. He stopped and smiled at her.

'She's got cold feet,' whispered Abigail. The man put his hand on the statue's foot.

'What she needs is some socks,' he said. 'Just like mine.' He pulled up his trouser legs and showed Abigail a pair of very bright red and yellow striped woolly socks. Abigail giggled.

'She's got something stuck in her toes,' she whispered. The man looked.

'Toffee paper,' he said, opening the piece of coloured shiny paper. 'That's a real silly place

to put it now. They should have stuck it up on the wall.'

'You don't stick toffee papers up in a Museum!' said Abigail. 'It's for pictures.'

'I like toffee papers,' said the man. 'You can go round looking at them and remembering what they all tasted like. I'll keep this one for my special collection.' He folded up the paper again and put it in his pocket.

Next day Abigail spent a long time in her bedroom. Nobody was allowed in until she was ready.

'Come and see,' she said at last. On the dressing table there was an old jam jar with one tiny tooth in the bottom. Hot Dog stood beside it trying very hard to look like a dinosaur. Stuck up on the mirror were three old toffee papers that Abigail had found in the waste paper basket.

'It's my Museum'' she said. 'You can come and look at my tooth if you like.'

'Very interesting,' said Mum. 'And a Dinosaur Dog as well, I see. But they don't have toffee papers in a Museum.'

'Yes they do so!' said Abigail. 'The man with the socks collects them specially – in his pockets.'

'Really!' said Mum. 'Well fancy that. You *do* learn something new every time you go to a Museum!'

2 Abigail and the Baby

Mum was talking to someone on the telephone.

'Of course he can come,' she said. 'We'd be delighted to have him.'

Abigail was sitting on the floor in the hall listening. She was rolling Paul's marbles up and down, trying to make them run through a cardboard tube.

'Who's coming?' she asked.

But Mum shook her head and went on talking. At last she put the telephone down.

'Right,' she said. 'We've got a job to do tomorrow, you and me. We're going to look after Christopher for Auntie Macdonald. She wants to go into town to do some shopping.'

Abigail had never looked after a real baby before.

'Can I play with him?' she asked.

'If you're careful,' said Mum. 'He's still very

little, and he can't run about yet.'

'What does he do then?' asked Abigail.

'He can crawl,' said Mum. 'He just hasn't learned how to walk yet.'

'Silly thing!' said Abigail. She crawled off down the hall, looking for Paul's marbles.

'Hmmmm,' said Mum.

Next morning Mum tidied up the living-room. She took the little china lady and the plants that stood on the window sill and put them up on a high shelf.

'Why did you do that?' said Abigail.

'Just in case,' said Mum. 'You never know with babies.'

'Would he want to play with them?' said Abigail.

'He might,' said Mum.

'That's silly,' said Abigail. 'I wasn't like that.'

She was digging through her toy box trying to find some toys that Christopher might like when the door-bell rang. It was Auntie Mac-donald with the pram.

'Ssshhhh,' said Mum, as Abigail came out to see. 'Christopher's asleep.'

Abigail looked into the pram. Christopher was lying on his back with his eyes closed. His face was very round and pink and his hair stood up in one little brown curl on top of his head.

'Hasn't he got up yet?' she whispered.

'He's only just gone to sleep!' said Auntie Macdonald. 'He's been up all night!'

'He's got very little hands,' said Abigail. 'Were my hands like that?'

'Course they were,' said Mum. 'And they used to be clean too!'

'When's he going to wake up?' said Abigail.

'When he wants to,' said Mum. 'You'll just have to play quietly for a while.'

Auntie Macdonald had a quick cup of coffee with Mum and then went off to catch a bus. Abigail took her trike and Hot Dog into the front garden.

'Shhhhh,' said Mum. 'Don't wake the baby.'

Abigail stopped pedalling and peeped into the pram. Christopher was still lying on his back, sound asleep. She went into the kitchen to watch Mum making the lunch.

'He's boring!' she said. 'He doesn't do any-thing.'

'Just wait!' said Mum. 'Pink pudding or chocolate?'

'Chocolate,' said Abigail. 'Can I make it?'

Mum put the milk and pudding mix in a bowl and Abigail mixed it up with a fork until the powder had gone and the milk was a thick smooth brown. They poured it into three bowls, one for Mum, one for Abigail, and a

20

little in the small blue baby bowl for Christopher.

'Just like the three bears,' said Abigail.

'Just like,' said Mum.

They left the pudding to set and sat down to watch Playschool on television. In the middle of the story, Christopher woke up.

'Waaaaaa!' he screamed. At first it was only a little scream, but then it became louder and louder until Abigail could hardly hear the story.

'Better go and see what's up,' said Mum.

Christopher's face was not pink any more. It was bright red. He was yelling and kicking, and all the pram covers were jumbled together. Abigail leaned over the pram.

'Poooooh!' she said. 'He's very smelly!'

'He needs a clean nappy,' said Mum. 'Hoot toot quick.' She took him into the bathroom, still kicking and yelling.

'He's very noisy,' said Abigail. She stood and watched while Mum changed the nappy.

'Pooooh!' she said. 'I wasn't like that.'

'Course you were, said Mum. 'Babies always are. Everyone is.'

'Even you? said Abigail. Mum nodded.

'And Dad – and Grandma and Grandad and everyone?' said Abigail.

'Of course,' said Mum. 'They all start off that size. She pulled a clean pair of pants on

21

Christopher and took him through to the living room. He sat on the floor and stared around him.

'Hello,' said Abigail, putting her face close up to him. He began to cry again. Mum picked him up and immediately he stopped crying. She bounced him on her knee and he smiled. Abigail laughed, and put out her hand.

'I'm Abigail,' she said. Christopher's podgy little fingers grabbed her hand.

'He wants to play with me,' she shouted. 'Look!'

Christopher stuffed Abigail's finger into his mouth.

'Yeouch!' she yelled. 'He bit me.'

'Fancy that,' said Mum. 'And he's only got one tooth too. He MUST be hungry.'

'Why's he only got one tooth?' asked Abigail, sucking her finger.

'Hasn't grown the rest yet,' said Mum. 'That's why he's a bit cross. It's not much fun growing teeth.'

'I grew all mine,' said Abigail making a wide mouth. 'Was I all cross?'

'Gruesome!' said Mum. 'Come on, let's give him something real to eat.'

Abigail sat on the stool at one side of the kitchen table and had beefburgers and chips for lunch. Mum sat on the other side with Christopher. She had some crispy biscuits with cheese. Christopher had a bowl of something white and sloppy.

'What's that?' said Abigail, staring at it.

'Gooey Gubbins,' said Mum. 'Babies like it.' She tied a bib round Christopher's neck and started to feed him with a plastic spoon. Abigail watched as he opened his little pink mouth and swallowed every mouthful.

'He's good at that,' she said.

'Goes like anything,' said Mum.

Just then Christopher squeezed his lips together and a long dribble of mush ran down his chin.

'Yuck,' said Abigail.

'Not a pretty sight,' said Mum, mopping him up. Christopher tried to grab the spoon, so Mum let him hold it with her.

'More?' she said.

'Yeeeeaaah,' yelled Christopher happily. He waved his other hand and brought it down SPLAT! in the middle of the white mush. Abigail, Mum and the table were covered in little white sticky blobs. Abigail started to giggle.

'Not funny,' said Mum. 'Get a cloth, quick.'

'Maybe he'd like a chip,' said Abigail when they had cleaned up. She held one out. Christopher grabbed it and shoved it into his mouth. He chewed right down the chip until all that was left was a little soggy dribbly bit. He

stretched out his hand and dropped that beside
Abigail's plate. She gave him another one. He
seemed to like them better than the white goo.
Abigail finished her beefburgers and Christopher dribbled through three more chips.

'Time for pud,' said Mum, and Abigail put
the plates of chocolate pudding on the table.

'I made that for you,' she said to Christopher.
He blew some very messy bubbles and wiped
a sticky handful of chips down her face.

'I think he likes you,' said Mum.

Abigail washed her face and came back to eat her pudding. Christopher was enjoying his. Sometimes the brown chocolate dribbles ran down to join the white dribbles on his bib, but most of it went inside.

'What a mess!' said Abigail giggling. 'Was I like that?'

'Much worse,' said Mum scraping some chocolate pudding off his chin with the spoon. Abigail laughed and dribbled a little pudding down her chin.

'But you're old enough to eat it properly now,' said Mum. 'Thank goodness.'

After lunch she put Christopher on the floor to crawl about while she did the washing up.

'Keep an eye on him,' she said. Christopher rolled over, crawled away and sat under the coffee table. Abigail lay on her tummy and tickled his feet. He laughed and rolled over.

'He's funny,' she shouted through to Mum.

'What was that?' called Mum.

'I said he's funny,' said Abigail, going to the kitchen door.

'Keep an eye on him,' said Mum. Abigail went back to see what he was doing.

'Oh help!' she shouted. Christopher had pulled Mum's magazine off the table and was tearing it apart. She tried to take it away but he screamed.

'Ah well,' said Mum. 'I had just about finished with it anyway.'

'Do you think he'd like something to play
with?' said Abigail, handing him Hot Dog.
Christopher grabbed Hot Dog by the leg and
threw his across the room. Abigail giggled and
gave him the small furry ball from his pram.

One after another all the toys were sent flying round the room. Mum came back through from the kitchen.

'There,' she said. 'That's the dishes done, and everything tidy.' And then she saw the mess.

'Ooo-er,' she said. Christopher threw away

the torn pages of the magazine and crawled off round the room dribbling soggy paper everywhere. Abigail rolled over beside him in among the muddle. They spent the whole afternoon playing together.

Christopher crawled everywhere! They had to put a chair in front of the television set and push the settee in front of the record player. He even tried to climb up the bookcase!

Abigail crawled around with him.

'Boo!' she shouted, popping out from behind an armchair. Christopher squealed with delight and pulled all the cushions off the seat, rolling over in among them. Abigail went to her bedroom to find some more toys for him to play with. When she came back, Mum was flopped into the big armchair. She had kicked off her shoes and was wriggling her toes. Abigail giggled.

'Shhhhh,' whispered Mum. Christopher was lying in the muddle of toys and torn paper on the floor sucking his thumb.

'I think he's actually tired!' whispered Mum. She lifted him out and tucked him into his pram.

By the time Auntie Macdonald came back Christopher was sound asleep, round and pink and rosy.

'He was quite happy then?' she whispered, peeping into the pram.

'Oh yes,' said Mum. 'I think he enjoyed himself.'

Mum and Abigail watched as Auntie Macdonald pushed the pram down the road.

'Would you like a baby like Christopher?' asked Abigail. 'For always?'

'Oh I don't know,' said Mum. 'They're very hard work.'

'Anyway you've got me and Paul,' said Abigail.

'Very true!' said Mum. 'And that's quite enough for anybody! Come on, let's go and tidy up before tea.'

3 Abigail and the Football Match

On Monday, Abigail bumped both her knees.

'Oh, good grief,' said Mum. 'Not again – that's the third time since Saturday. What happened?'

'I was helping Hot Dog down,' said Abigail, watching Mum clean up the dirt.

'Down?' said Mum. 'Where was he?'

'On the shed roof,' said Abigail. 'Can I have stickies on my knees?'

'Honestly Abigail!' said Mum. 'Why don't you go and do a jigsaw puzzle on the floor. You can't fall off that. And do try to play a game that keeps your knees clean!'

On Tuesday, Abigail and Mum went to visit Pete from the Playgroup. Pete took Abigail out to the garden.

'I've got a police car,' he said. He opened the shed door and pulled it out.

'That's not a police car,' said Abigail. 'It's an old box with wheels.'

'It's a police car!' shouted Pete.

' 'Tis not!' shouted Abigail.

'Keep the noise down, you two,' called Pete's Mum from the window. 'We can't hear ourselves speak.'

'It's a police car,' said Pete quietly. He sat in the box and pushed himself along with his feet, making a police car noise.

'See!' he said.

'I'll push you,' said Abigail. Very soon they were racing round and round the garden making police car noises.

'Stop it!' yelled Abigail's Mum from the window. 'And play quietly.' They tried to play police cars more quietly but it was difficult. Pete's Mum had to pop her head out twice more to tell them to make less noise.

'Honestly Abigail,' said Mum, on the way home, 'nobody likes all that screaming and shouting. You must learn to play quietly.'

'Boring!' said Abigail.

On Wednesday, Abigail went down the road to bake cakes with Angela. They made little cakes, and big cakes, round cakes and square cakes, cakes in yoghurt pots, and cakes in old ice-cream tubs. They were all a beautiful dark brown colour, just like real ones, and were decorated with stones and sticks and leaves.

'Crikey!' said Mum, when Abigail went

home. 'What happened?'

'We were making cakes,' said Abigail. She looked down at her dungerees. They were covered in thick sticky mud. She wiped her hands down the front.

'Don't do that,' said Mum, and bundled

Abigail straight into a bath.

'Honestly Abigail,' she said. 'You must learn to play without getting so filthy dirty!'

On Thursday, it poured with rain.

'Why can't I go out to play?' asked Abigail, for the tenth time that morning.

'Because you can't,' said Mum. 'It's bucketing down out there. Honestly Abigail, nobody goes out to play in the rain.'

'Boring,' said Abigail, breathing on the steamy window pane.

On Friday, Paul came racing in from school. He threw his bag and anorak on the floor.

'I'm in the football team!' he shouted. 'You'll all have to come and watch tomorrow.'

'Great!' said Mum.

'We'll all come and cheer,' said Dad.

'Football's boring,' said Abigail. 'I'm not going.'

'Yes, you are!' said Mum.

Next morning, Mum packed Paul's clean red and white top and his white shorts and football boots in a bag. The boots were polished and shining with new white laces.

Dad was down on his knees looking for something in the Muddle Cupboard in the hall. He pulled out boxes and boots and old baskets full of things.

'What are you doing?' said Mum.

'It's here somewhere,' said Dad. 'I know it is.

And we can't go to a football game without it.'

'What is it?' said Abigail, who was standing behind him, watching.

'Aha!' said Dad. He sat back on the floor and pulled out something that looked like a wooden flag with a handle.

'It's my old rackety,' he said, and swung it round his head. Rackety-rackety-clackety-clackety. The noise was amazing!

'I want to do that!' shouted Abigail. She swung it round and round above her head until Mum came through to see what was going on.

'I think we'd better keep it for the game,' said Dad, taking it back. 'I always used to take it to football when I was small. You can carry it, Abigail.'

Abigail couldn't wait to get to the football game. They walked round to the field behind the school. Paul and his friends went off to change inside the school. Mum, Dad and Abigail found a place to stand among all the other people who had come to watch the game.

'It's a bit wet still,' said Mum. 'Just as well we wore our wellies.'

Abigail jumped up and down on the grass and the water squeezed out round her yellow boots, just like the sponge in the bath.

'It's very muddy,' she said, rocking backwards and forwards. Her boots made a lovely squelching sound.

'It is a bit,' said Mum, but she didn't seem to mind.

'Here they come!' shouted someone, and the boys ran out on to the field. There was Paul's team in red and white tops, and the other team in blue tops. They all wore very clean white shorts and shining football boots, and looked very smart.

The crowd round the football pitch shouted and cheered. Abigail swung the rackety round her head.

A man in a black top and shorts came on with a ball. He dropped it in the middle of the field, blew a whistle, and off raced the boys, kicking the ball.

'Come on!' yelled Dad, waving.

'Kick it Paul!' shouted Mum at the top of her voice. She was jumping up and down on the squelchy grass. All around Abigail, people were jumping about and shouting. She could hardly hear the rackety.

'Go on!' they yelled.

'Watch your back!' shouted others. The boys on the field shouted to each other and raced about on the muddy grass.

'Mind that ball!' yelled Dad, as it bounced towards the goal posts. As Paul ran out and kicked the ball away, he tripped and skidded across the muddy grass.

'Great save!' shouted Mum, waving her

hands in the air. Abigail stared in horror.

'Look at his knees!' she said, but Mum didn't hear her; she wasn't listening.

'His knees!' she shouted, pulling at Mum's coat.

'Oh never mind that,' said Mum. 'Come on!'

The boys raced off down the field, chasing the ball as it bounced across the wet grass. They pushed and shoved and shouted, tripping over each other.

'They're very noisy,' yelled Abigail, but no-

body heard her in the cheering and shouting.

'Get that ball,' yelled the man behind them.
The boys tumbled over each other in a jumble
of arms and legs. The ball flew up over their
heads and into the goal. The crowd yelled with
delight and the man in the black top and shorts
blew his whistle.

'It's a goal!' shouted Dad, swinging Abigail
up in the air. 'Paul's team are winning.'

Abigail swung the rackety round and round
above her head making as much noise as she

possibly could. The boys sorted themselves out and ran back to the centre of the field.

Abigail stopped swinging the rackety.

'Look at them!' she said. They were absolutely covered in mud. The clean white shorts were quite black and their legs and knees were thick with it. Their boots looked as if they had walked through chocolate pudding. Even their hands and faces were filthy.

'They're mucky,' shouted Abigail, but nobody listened. The boys had kicked off and were racing back down the field after the ball again.

Abigail felt something cold and wet on her nose. She looked up. The sky was dark and grey and very slowly it started to rain huge wet drops. She pulled up the hood of her anorak and pulled her hands up inside the sleeves. Out on the field the rain made muddy streaks down the boys' legs as they raced after the ball. It lay in puddles round the goals, but nobody seemed to mind. They cheered and shouted just the same.

'Are we going home now?' said Abigail.

'Why?' shouted Dad. 'Aren't you enjoying it?'

'It's raining,' said Abigail.

'Oh, it's only a little bit,' said Mum. 'It's not that wet.'

The boys played on and on. After a time

they stopped for a rest, changed goals and played another game. The blue team raced up and scored a goal. Paul tried to stop them but he slipped and fell in a puddle. Abigail looked up at Mum.

'That's a shame,' said Mum. 'He'd have stopped that if it hadn't been raining.' She didn't seem to have noticed that he was soaking wet as well as muddy.

The boys chased each other up and down the field. The rain fell heavier than ever and at last they all became so muddy it was hard to tell which one was Paul. It was even difficult to tell which tops were blue and which were red and white.

At last the man in the black shorts and top blew his whistle. He was the only one who was not covered in mud.

Everyone cheered and the boys ran off the field into the school.

'That's it,' said Dad. 'We can go home now. Did you enjoy it?'

'Yes!' said Abigail, swinging the rackety above her head. 'It was great.'

'Do you think you'd like to be a football supporter?' said Mum, 'and come and watch more games?'

'No,' said Abigail, watching the boys stamping off in their very muddy boots. 'I want to be a football player.'

4 Abigail Can't Sleep

'I can't sleep,' shouted Abigail from the bed-room.

'Course you can,' said Mum, sticking her head round the door. 'You're just not trying hard enough.'

'I want the lights off,' said Abigail.

'Not just at the moment,' said Mum. 'Paul's still reading.'

Paul, in the other bed, was reading through a huge pile of old comics which he had borrowed from a friend at school.

'Look,' said Mum. 'Turn round on your other side and pull the quilt up over your head to make a little dark cave. Then you'll get to sleep.'

Abigail humped around in the bed.

'For goodness sake!' she muttered from beneath the blankets.

'What's wrong now?' asked Mum.

'Stupid hot water bottle!' said Abigail. She pulled the quilt up over her head and disappeared. Mum tiptoed around the bedroom for a few minutes picking up socks from the floor, tidying clothes, and straightening the books on the book shelf.

'Better put the light off now,' she whispered. Paul put his pile of comics on the table beside the bed and switched off the light.

'Good night,' whispered Mum, tiptoeing to the door.

'I can't sleep,' muttered the hump on Abigail's bed.

'Sssshh,' said Mum. 'The light's off now. It's quite dark, so you can settle down.'

'I've still got my eyes open,' said Abigail.

'No use looking in the dark,' said Paul. 'Your batteries will go flat.'

Abigail giggled.

'You're stupid,' she said. 'I don't have batteries.'

'Be quiet the pair of you,' said Mum. 'Not another word.'

Paul humped round in his bed and settled down. Abigail lay still in the dark, with her eyes wide open.

The light from the hall made shadows with the bumpy patterns on the wallpaper. It looked a bit like the sand on a beach when the tide goes out. Abigail thought about the picnics she had had on the beach last summer. It had been very hot, and bright, and there had been lots to eat and drink.

'Can I have an orange juice?' she called out. Mum popped her head round the door.

'Nope,' she said. 'You finished it all at teatime, remember? Now go to sleep.'

'But I'm thirsty,' said Abigail. 'Please can I have a drink – please?'

'All right,' said Mum. She brought a glass of water.

'Now that's it!' she said. 'Settle down and go to sleep.'

Abigail lay quietly in the dark for a few minutes.

'Mum!' she shouted.

'What is it now?' said Mum.

'I want to go to the bathroom,' shouted Abigail.

'If you must, you must,' sighed Mum. Abigail went to the bathroom.

While she was there she had a sniff at the pink bath cubes, squeezed the water slowly out of the bath sponge, and made faces at her reflection in the shiny bath taps. It was funny because it made her face look very fat at the top and long and thin at the bottom.

She was wobbling on the bathroom scales when Mum came through.

'Bed!' she said. 'Hop it! Right now!'

Abigail went back to bed.

'I can't sleep,' she grumbled, settling back down under the covers.

'How do you know, if you haven't even tried?' said Mum, tucking her in. 'Think about something nice. A princess in a pink dress.'

Abigail lay in the dark and thought about a princess in a pink dress. It was a pink and silver dress, like the picture in her Cinderella story book. There were shiny ribbons and little bunches of flowers pinned on the skirt.

'Wish I had a dress like that,' thought Abigail. Then she thought about the princess's bedroom. It would be beautiful – and tidy – with no socks on the floor. There were lace curtains, and a four poster bed, with a pink shiny quilt, and the princess would have a teddy bear . . .

Abigail sat up in bed suddenly.

'Mum!' she yelled. 'I haven't got Hot Dog.'

Abigail never, ever, went to bed without Hot Dog.

'Shhhhh,' whispered Mum, coming back into the bedroom. 'You'll wake Paul. Where is Hot Dog anyway?'

'Down the back of the settee,' said Abigail. 'It's his new house.'

'I might have known,' said Mum. She went off and came back a minute later with a rather dusty Hot Dog.

'Now will you go to sleep?' she asked.

'No,' said Abigail. 'I can't sleep. I'm going to stay awake all night. Right till breakfast time.'

'Go on!' said Mum. 'I bet you can't.'

'Can too!' said Abigail.

'Right, let's see you do it then,' said Mum.

Abigail snuggled down in bed, holding Hot Dog's ear against her nose. Her thumb was tired so she stuck it in her mouth.

'Good night,' whispered Mum.

'Good night,' muttered Abigail. It sounded funny with her thumb plugged in.

Mum tiptoed out of the bedroom. Abigail stretched – and yawned – and went to sleep.

5 Abigail's Pocket Money

It was Saturday morning and that meant pocket-money day.

Abigail sat at the breakfast table, finishing her orange juice and looking at the shiny silver ten pence lying on the cloth beside her. She stared at the picture of the Queen for a long time.

'That's not a proper crown,' she said.

'That's just a little one she keeps for sitting about on pennies,' said Dad. 'What are you going to do with it?'

'Don't know,' said Abigail. She turned the ten pence over and looked at the other side.

'The lion's wearing a proper crown,' she said. 'Why's the lion got a crown and the Queen hasn't?'

'Finish your breakfast,' said Mum. 'And don't talk so much.'

Dad disappeared behind the newspaper.

Abigail finished her eggs and took the plate through to the kitchen.

'Can I spend my pocket money now?' she asked.

'Wait till I'm going shopping,' said Mum. 'You can come with me.'

'I want to go on my own, to the shop at the corner,' said Abigail. 'Please?'

'Ask your Dad,' said Mum. 'If he thinks you're big enough to go on your own, then it's all right.'

Dad was in the front garden cutting the grass.

'I'm big enough,' said Abigail. 'Can I go to the corner and spend my money myself?'

'Well ... I suppose so,' said Dad. 'But you mustn't cross the road, remember.'

'I won't,' said Abigail.

'I could go with her,' said Paul.

'No!' said Abigail. 'I want to go on my own.'

'All right,' said Dad. 'But straight there and straight back. OK?'

'OK,' said Abigail, and she zipped her ten pence into the top pocket of her dungarees.

'Goodbye,' she said to Mum. 'I won't be long.'

'Have a good time,' said Mum.

Abigail went to the front gate and stood looking down the road.

'What are you going to buy?' asked Paul. He was helping Dad with the lawnmower.

'Crisps,' said Abigail, swinging on the gate.
'And a pencil, and a book to write in and a
comic.'

'You can't get all those with ten pence!' said
Paul.

'Bet I can,' said Abigail. She swung on the
gate for a while watching Dad oiling the lawnmower. She looked down the street. There
were people walking up to the shops. In another garden, a lawnmower was already buzz-
ing. Across the road, a man was polishing his
car.

'Still here then?' said Dad looking up.

Abigail ran back into the house.

'Hello,' said Mum. 'That was quick.'

'Haven't been yet,' said Abigail. 'Hot Dog
want to come too.'

'Good idea,' said Mum. 'I think he'd like a
walk.'

Hot Dog was lying in a heap with Abigail's
pyjamas on the floor. She picked them up,
shook out Hog Dog and stuffed the pyjamas
under her pillow.

'Bye again,' called Mum.

'Bye,' shouted Abigail. She cuddled Hot
Dog under her arm and stuffed her hands in
behind the top of her dungarees.

'Bye,' said Dad. He stood and watched as
Abigail skipped off down the road, singing to
herself.

'I'll keep an eye on her,' he called to Mum.

Abigail hadn't gone very far when she came to Mr. Campbell's gate. It looked very shiny, and had a funny smell. Abigail was just about to touch it when Mr. Campbell's head popped up from behind the hedge.

'Don't do that,' he said. 'Wet paint.'

'It's a funny colour,' said Abigail.

'Do you think so?' said Mr. Campbell. He stood back and looked at it. 'I hadn't enough, so I just mixed two or three pots together. I found them in the garage.'

'I'm going shopping myself,' said Abigail, 'with all my pocket money. I'm going to buy some crisps, a comic, a pencil, and a book to write in.'

'That reminds me,' said Mr. Campbell. 'Don't go away.'

He put down the pot of paint and went back into the house. Abigail and Hot Dog stood and waited. She reached out a finger tip and just touched the gate to see if it really was wet. She was just wiping her finger clean on the hedge when Mr. Campbell came out again.

'Here you are,' he said. 'Found it the other day. I just thought to myself, I know someone who'd like that.'

He handed Abigail a little red plastic book with gold letters on the cover.

'It's an old diary,' he said. 'And it even has a pencil.'

Down the back of the diary was a round hole, and in the hole was a very thin red pencil with a little white hat on the end. The hat stopped the pencil from sliding right through and out at the bottom.

'You can write down all the things you do', said Mr. Campbell. 'There's even a place at the back to put your friends' names and where they live.'

Abigail tried the pencil. It worked perfectly. Mr. Campbell wrote her name at the top of the first page so that everyone would know that it was her book. Abigail zipped it into her top pocket with the ten pence.

'Thank you very much,' she said.

'Not at all,' said Mr. Campbell. 'My pleasure.'

'I like your gate,' said Abigail, 'really.'

'Good of you to say so,' said Mr. Campbell. He went back to painting again.

Abigail's friend Angela was sitting on her front door step in the sunshine, reading.

'Look,' she shouted. 'I've got *two* comics! My Mum bought one, and then Gran came over this morning and she's brought another one the same.'

'I've got a secret in my pocket,' said Abigail. 'Something special. It was a present.'

'Let me see, and I'll give one of my comics,' said Angela.

'All right,' said Abigail. She opened the pocket and took out the little book. She showed Angela the pencil and let her take it out.

'I could put your name in my book,' she said. 'What is it?'

'You know what it is,' said Angela. Abigail giggled and pretended to write it in the book.

'Now I have to write where you live,' she said.

'Here,' said Angela, but Abigail didn't know how to write that.

'I'm going to spend my ten pence,' she said. 'Are you coming with me?'

Angela shook her head so Abigail took her comic, folded it up very small and stuffed it into her pocket with the red book and the ten pence.

'Bye,' she said, and skipped off down the road to the shop.

She was just passing the last house when old Mrs. Paterson waved to her from the front door.

'Abigail,' she called. 'Are you going to the shops?'

'I'm going to spend my ten pence,' called Abigail. 'All on my own with Hot Dog.'

'Good for you,' said Mrs. Paterson. 'I

wonder if you could post some letters for me.
Just pop them in the box at the corner.' She
had three letters with stamps stuck on them.

Abigail skipped up to the letter box. She
stood on tiptoe to try and see inside, but it was
very dark in there. She dropped the letters in
and heard them fall on the others in the box.

'Hoooooo!' she said into the slot. Her voice
sounded funny inside the letter box. She held
on very tightly to Hot Dog, just in case he
wanted to jump in too, and went into the
newspaper shop.

There were boxes all along the counter with crisps in them. Abigail always took a long time deciding which bag she wanted.

'Eeny meeny minie mo,' she counted. But she still couldn't decide. She looked all round the shop at the rows of coloured shiny magazines and the piles of newspapers on the counter.

A big brown shaggy dog came in on its own.

'Hello,' said the woman behind the counter. The dog put its front paws up on the edge, its tongue hanging out, dribbling on the papers. The woman folded a newspaper and put it in his mouth. The dog wagged its tail and went back out again. Abigail stood at the door and watched it go up the road carrying the paper.

'You couldn't do that,' she said to Hot Dog. Hot Dog said nothing.

'Can I help you?' said the lady behind the counter. Abigail chose some cheese and onion crisps and handed over the ten pence.

She skipped back up the road. Mrs. Paterson waved from the front path.

'Did you post them?' she called.

'Yes,' said Abigail. 'All of them.'

'You are clever,' Mrs. Paterson said, and she gave Abigail a shiny silver ten pence.

'Thank you,' said Abigail, and put it in her top pocket with the little book, and the comic.

Angela was still sitting on her doorstep, so

they sat together, ate the crisps and played with Hot Dog.

'Did you have a good time?' Dad asked, when she went home.

'What did you get?' asked Paul.

Abigail unzipped the top pocket of her dungarees. She pulled out the little red book with the pencil, the comic, the empty crisp bag, and the silver ten pence.

'How did you get all that?' said Paul.

'Easy peasy,' said Abigail, and she went inside to tell Mum.

6 Abigail at the Park

Abigail's Dad was building a boat.

'It's very small,' said Abigail.

'It's only a model,' said Dad. He was very slowly and carefully painting a thin gold line along the side.

'Why does it have brown sails?' said Abigail.

'Because I like them,' said Dad. 'And don't bump the table.'

'Will it work?' said Abigail.

'Course it will,' said Dad, sitting back and looking at the boat. 'I can play with it in my bath.'

'It's too big!' Abigail giggled. 'There wouldn't be any room for you.'

'Maybe you're right,' said Dad. 'We could take it to the park though. It would sail in the boating pond.'

'Can we go now?' said Abigail, bouncing up and down.

'No,' said Dad. 'It's nearly bedtime. But I tell you what, Mum's going into town tomorrow to buy a new dress, so you and me and Paul could go to the park instead.'

'What a very good idea!' said Mum.

In the morning Dad packed the camera and a picnic bag.

'Orange juice, apples, biscuits, egg sandwiches ...'

'You'd better take spare socks and shoes,' said Mum.

'What for?' said Dad.

'Somebody's bound to fall in the pond,' she said. 'And there's nothing worse than wet feet.'

'Nobody's going to fall in when I'm in charge!' said Dad, but Mum put in spare socks and shoes for Paul and Abigail – just in case.

The park was quite busy. There were children playing on the swings, a crowd round the ice-cream van, and over by the pond a line of people were waiting to hire rowing boats.

'Can we have our picnic now?' said Abigail. 'On the grass beside the daffodils?'

'No!' said Paul. 'We've only just got here!'

'We'll have a look round first,' said Dad. 'And see what's what.' They left the picnic bag and the boat in the car, took the camera with them, and went for a walk round the park.

Abigail had a long play on the swings.

'I like the one with the blue seat best,' she said. 'It's the fastest. Go on, push it again Dad.'

'Oh, come on!' said Dad. 'I'm puffed out pushing you. Let's look at something else.'

'I want to stay here,' said Abigail.

Dad wandered off up a path between high dark green bushes. Paul went on ahead of him.

'Wait for me!' shouted Abigail. She jumped down and ran after them. The bushes were very high, and there were trees among them. It was quite dark walking up the path.

'Do you think there are wolves in here?' she whispered.

'No chance,' said Dad. 'It's too noisy for them round here.'

'What's that?' whispered Abigail. They stood still and listened.

'I don't know,' said Dad. 'It came from the bushes. Let's go and see.'

'I don't want to,' said Abigail, holding his hand very tightly. 'What if it's a wolf?'

'Shhhh,' said Dad. They tiptoed off the path and round the back of one of the thick bushes.

'Look at that,' whispered Dad. 'He's a funny sort of wolf.'

Abigail stared. The little furry animal on the ground sat up and stared back at her with bright shiny eyes. His long tail and pointed

ears stood straight up as if he was very surprised to see them. Then he picked up a nut
and stuffed it into his mouth.

'It's a squirrel,' said Dad. 'Having a picnic.'

The squirrel rummaged about on the
ground and started to stuff another nut into its
mouth.

'Shocking table manners,' whispered Dad.
'I wonder what its Mum would say.' Abigail
giggled, the squirrel dropped the nut and ran
straight up the trunk of a tree.

'Will he come back?'' said Abigail, staring
up into the branches.

'He will if we go away,' said Dad. 'Come
on, I think it's time we had our picnic.'

They walked on down the path back to the car.

'I like the flowers,' said Abigail. She stopped to look at a pale pink clump of blossoms on one of the dark green bushes. 'Angela's Gran's got a hat like that. Do you think Mum'll get one?'

'Shouldn't think so,' said Dad. 'Tell you what though, you stand beside the bush and I'll take a picture. We'll make it look as if you're wearing some flowers as a hat.'

Abigail stood underneath a huge pink clump of flowers. Dad arranged them right on top of her head and brushed her fringe straight.

'Smile please!' he said. Abigail turned up her nose and smiled like a very posh lady at a wedding.

'What on earth are you doing?' said Paul, coming back to look for them.

'I'm going to a wedding!' sang Abigail. She bounced out of the bush and a shower of little pink flowers fell around her like confetti. There were others already lying scattered around on the ground.

'Can I keep some?' said Abigail.

'Course,' said Dad, so she filled the pocket of her anorak with the pink flowers.

'I'm hungry,' said Paul.

'OK' said Dad. 'Time for lunch.'

They took the picnic bag and the model

boat to a bench beside the pond. Abigail ate most of her sandwiches. She kept the crusts for the ducks who came over from the island in the middle to see what they were doing.

'There's a little one that's not getting any,' she shouted. She leaned over to try and throw the bread further out.

'Careful,' shouted Dad. He jumped up, knocking over his orange juice.

'It's all down your trousers!' said Paul.

Dad grabbed the first thing he could find to mop up.

'That's my clean socks!' shouted Abigail.

'Well just don't get your feet wet,' said Dad. He stuffed the socks back in the bag and went to help feed the ducks. A huge white shaggy dog bounced down the path, and the ducks scattered and flew off as it jumped into the pond and raced towards them.

'Watch out!' said Dad and Abigail dodged behind him.

'Come here, boy! Come here! Sit, sit!' shouted a large lady in a raincoat, who was running along behind the dog. But the dog splashed and bounced about in the water and wagged his tail. Abigail laughed and clapped her hands.

'Come out of that, Benjamin!' shouted the lady. The huge shaggy dog stopped barking, jumped out of the water and started to shake

itself. A shower of raindrops flew through the air.

'I'm most awfully sorry,' said the lady. 'Are you terribly wet?'

'Not too bad,' said Dad, brushing down his wet jersey. 'I'll dry out.'

'He's lovely!' said Abigail, patting the dog's nose. They stood and watched as it bounced off down the path leaving huge wet footprints.

'Can we have one like that?' said Paul.

'Hmmph,' said Dad, rubbing his hands on

his jersey. 'Come on, let's go and sail this boat before anything else daft happens.'

Very carefully, he knelt down and put the boat in the water. A puff of wind filled the brown sails and it bobbed off across the waves.

'It looks real,' shouted Abigail, running along the path beside it.

'Don't you need a string so it won't sail away?' said Paul.

'No,' said Dad. 'The wind will bring it back to the edge of the pond. We'll just walk round and catch it wherever it comes ashore.'

The tiny boat sailed backwards and forwards across the pond, in between the ducks and the big rowing boats. Paul and Dad pulled the sails tighter so that it went faster, then they moved the rudder to make it sail in circles. Abigail made a daisy chain that hung from the top of the mast like a string of flags.

'It's beginning to get stormy!' shouted Paul. It was colder and the tiny ripples on the water were becoming waves. A wind blew across the park, chasing round the tree tops and dancing through the daffodils.

'Last time, I think,' said Dad. 'It's not as warm as it was.' He pushed the boat out from the bank. The wind caught the brown sails and it swung round.

'It's going to get stuck on the ducks' island,' yelled Paul, running along the path.

'No, it's not,' said Dad. But it did. The little boat jammed itself under the branches of a bush that grew on the island.

'We'll have to get a rowing boat and rescue it,' said Dad, and they walked round to the hut where the people had been waiting to hire boats.

'Er – my son's lost his boat,' said Dad to the lady in the ticket office. 'We'll have to go out for it.'

'I thought that might happen,' said the lady. She didn't look up; she was counting the stitches in her knitting. Abigail stared at her. She wore a long black duffel coat and wellingtons. A white frilly blouse stuck out round the neck and her black curly hair was stuffed into a red knitted pom-pom hat. When she looked up her golden ear-rings jingled.

'That's one and two halves,' she said, handing Dad the tickets. 'And mind what you're doing, you two. We don't want anyone falling in.'

'They'll be all right with me,' said Dad. He put Abigail at the front of the boat and Paul at the back, and sat in the middle with the oars.

'She's a funny lady,' whispered Abigail as they slid out across the water.

'Shhhh,' said Dad. 'She'll hear you.' He looked back at the lady who was standing watching them.

'Maybe she's a retired pirate,' he whispered and pulled on the oars.

It was difficult to get the rowing boat close to the bush. The water was not quite deep enough.

'Can you reach it, Abigail?' he said, but Abigail's arms were not long enough. He turned the boat round to see if Paul could reach it, but that was no use either. He tried to stretch out with one of the oars, but the little boat was stuck firmly in the bush.

'Nothing for it,' said Dad. 'I'll have to climb over and get it.' He tied the boat to a tree and stepped on to the island.

'Can we come too?' shouted Abigail.

'Better not,' said Dad. 'And don't move about in that boat. Sit still where I can see you.' He climbed round the bushes and reached out to the little boat.

'Got it!' he shouted. His feet slipped on a wet stone.

Splash! He was up to his knees in very cold water.

He stood and stared down at his feet sinking into the dirty brown mud and shook his head.

'These shoes must be letting in water,' he said. 'My feet are getting wet.'

Paul and Abigail looked at each other and started to giggle.

Dad was sitting on the park bench trying to

squeeze the water out of his socks when Mum
came down the path to meet them.

'Did you have a good time?' she asked, as
Paul and Abigail came running up. 'How did
the boat go?'

'Great!' said Paul. 'It goes dead fast!'

'And you managed to keep your feet dry,'
said Mum, looking at their socks and shoes.
'That's quite something.'

Then she saw Dad.

'Oh no!' she said. Dad held up his wet socks and nodded.

'Honestly,' said Mum. 'I don't believe it. You're worse than the pair of them.' And they all sat on the park bench and laughed.

7 Abigail's New Bedroom

Paul and Abigail were arguing about the bedroom again.

'It's your turn to tidy it up,' said Paul. 'It's mostly your junk on the floor.'

'Is not!' shouted Abigail. 'Anyway you put it there!'

'Oh, get on with it and stop arguing' said Mum. 'You could have been finished by now.'

Abigail tidied up her end of the room and Paul tidied up his. When Mum came through there was one of Abigail's socks lying on the floor in Paul's end and a pair of his slippers lying in Abigail's end.

'I'm not touching his smelly old slippers!' said Abigail.

'Pooh! Stinky socks,' said Paul, pushing Abigail's sock with his toe, so Mum picked them up.

'You two,' she said, 'would be better off in a couple of cages at the zoo!'

But Dad had a better idea when he came home.

'Give them a room each,' he said.

'What a good idea,' said Mum. 'We could make a bedroom up in the loft. It's big enough, and there's a lot of junk up there that could be thrown out.'

'No!' said Abigail. 'I like it. That's my house!'

The loft had a secret entrance that looked like an ordinary cupboard door in the hall. When you opened it, instead of coats and vacuum cleaners and junk falling out, like the other hall cupboard, there was a staircase inside. The stairs were very high, and squeezed together. Halfway up they turned round a corner. At the top was a big square room that sloped up on all four sides into the roof. It was quite dark in the corners because there were only three small skylight windows.

When it was very hot in the summer they had to be opened to let fresh air in because the loft was very stuffy.

Abigail liked the loft. It was full of old toys and all sorts of things that had been stuffed into boxes and put upstairs out of the way.

'Can I have it for my bedroom?' she asked.

'I wanted it,' said Paul. 'You have the

69

downstairs bedroom.' That started another argument.

On the first week-end when Dad had some time off he opened all the windows and started to clear out the loft. He threw out old books and magazines, bits of carpet, and filled up bags of rubbish. Under the spare bed was an old white hairy rug.

'That's the carpet for my house,' wailed Abigail. 'I need it.'

'It's mucky!' said Mum.

'We could always clean it up a bit,' said Dad and he put the rug to one side.

'Fancy that,' said Mum when she found some old plates in a corner. 'We used to have a whole tea-set of those.'

'They're my dishes,' said Abigail. 'Can I keep them?'

'Oh well – I suppose so,' said Mum. 'They were a nice tea-set.' She put the plates into a cardboard box to go downstairs.

'Well, look at this,' said Dad. He pulled out a picture of a sailing ship. 'I had that in my room when I was the same age as Paul.'

'I want that,' said Abigail. 'That's the picture for my house.'

'It's horrible!' said Mum. 'It's gone a funny colour. You can't possibly like that!'

'Oh – let's keep it,' said Dad. And it went in the pile to go downstairs.

They worked on all day until at last the loft was almost empty and all that was left stood in a little pile in one corner. The room looked very big and dark and the spare bed looked quite lonely in the corner by itself. There were squares of brightness on the floor where the sun shone in the skylights. Mum swept up and Abigail watched the tiny specks of dust dancing in the light.

'Do you want to sleep up here tonight?' said Mum. 'Or wait till we've painted it?'

'Wait till it's painted,' said Paul and Abigail together.

Mum and Dad worked all the next day, painting the loft white. They put down some rugs, and a small table with a lamp on it beside the bed.

'Right,' said Dad. 'Who's going to have it for a bedroom?'

'Why not take it in turns?' said Mum. 'Paul can have it tonight because he's bigger, and Abigail can have it tomorrow night.'

So that night Paul slept up in the loft.

'It's not fair,' muttered Abigail, stumping off to her own bed downstairs.

'Your turn tomorrow,' said Mum. 'Just wait.'

Next morning Abigail went out to play in the garden.

'Is it time for bed yet?' she asked, when

71

Mum made her an orange juice.

'No,' said Mum. 'You've only just got up. Come and help me wash the old plates we found upstairs. You can have lunch on one of them.'

'Is it time for bed yet?' Abigail asked after lunch.

'Not yet,' said Mum. 'You're a big girl now, you don't need a sleep in the afternoon. Come and help me clean the shaggy old rug from the loft.'

'Is it time for bed yet?' Abigail asked, standing in front of the television set.

'Yes,' said Paul. 'I can't see through you.'

'Do you want to go just now?' said Mum, 'or have your tea first?'

'No,' said Abigail. 'I want my tea.'

'Well then, don't be daft,' said Mum.

After tea Abigail had a bath. She came through from the bathroom in her nightgown, trailing Hot Dog behind her.

'Is it . . .?'

'YES!' shouted Mum and Dad and Paul all together.

Abigail climbed up the secret stair to the bed in the loft. She had never been up there at night before. The little lamp on the table made shadows up in the high pointed roof. It was very dark in the corners.

'Would you like a story?' said Dad.

'Yes,' said Abigail. Dad sat on the edge of the bed and told a three bears story. Usually she liked it when he told the three bears because he pretended to be a huge growly father bear. He made a deep roaring growling voice.

'Tell a mother bear story tonight,' said Abigail.

'All right,' said Dad, and he told the story quietly in a mother bear voice.

'Time for lights out,' he said at the end. 'OK?'

'OK,' said Abigail. She slid down and pulled the covers right up to her nose. Dad put out the light and crept off downstairs.

Abigail peeped out. It was quite different in the loft at night. It was dark outside and there were no curtains on the skylight windows. She could see the clouds like floppy grey cotton-wool slowly sliding past the window. There was one that looked a little bit like a face. Abigail slid down under the covers again. Hot Dog was down there.waiting for a cuddle. She could feel his nose poking into her, but she couldn't see him in the dark. When she slept downstairs, Mum always left the door open so that the light from the hall shone in.

'Mum!' she shouted.

'What is it?' called Mum from the bottom of the stairs.

'Can you leave the secret door open and the light on?' shouted Abigail.

'It is on,' called Mum. 'You can't see it because you're upstairs.'

Abigail snuggled down and cuddled Hot Dog's ear to her nose.

Scritch, scratch, scritch. It sounded as if something was walking on the roof!

'Mum!' she shouted. 'Mum, there's a monster!'

Mum and Dad came running up the stairs. Dad put the light on and looked around.

'Nothing here,' he said. 'Just you and Hot Dog.'

'I heard it!' shouted Abigail. 'It was walking on the roof.'

It must have been the birds,' Mum laughed. 'They live up here too. It's their house as well.'

Then Abigail remembered that sometimes when she played in her house she could hear the birds singing just above her head on the top of the roof. She had never noticed the scritch scratch noise their feet made.

'Settle down,' said Dad. 'Go to sleep and you won't hear anything.'

He and Mum went back downstairs again.

Abigail was lying in the dark, all curled up and nearly asleep when suddenly there was a horrible gurgling noise just behind her bed.

'Mum!' she screamed, sitting up in bed. 'Mum!'

The horrible gurgling noise changed to a thump, thump, thump. It sounded like feet.

'Mum!' yelled Abigail.

'Coming,' shouted Mum. She tripped on the stairs on her long night-gown.

'Bother!' she said.

'Mum,' yelled Abigail. 'There's SOME-THING!'

Mum stood in the middle of the loft and listened. The gurgling was quieter now, as if it was going away. There was a little hissing sound following it.

'It's a snake,' whispered Abigail.

'Oh Abigail,' said Mum, 'it's only the hot water running round the pipes. Dad's having a bath. He's just down beneath you.'

'I don't like it!' said Abigail, holding tight to Hot Dog.

'Do you want to sleep downstairs?' said Mum. Abigail nodded her head.

'Come on,' said Mum. They took Hot Dog and Abigail's dressing gown and went back down to the bedroom where Paul was sound asleep in his own bed.

'Shhh,' said Mum, tucking Abigail in. 'Now go to sleep.'

Next morning Paul was very surprised to wake up and find Abigail downstairs.

'Scaredy cat,' he said.

'Am not,' said Abigail. 'Hot Dog didn't like it. He says you can have the stupid old loft. We're going to make a house in the bedroom with my rug and beautiful picture and everything.'

Paul packed all his books and toys and model planes into a box.

'It's much better already,' said Mum, looking round the tidy bedroom. She helped him carry them up to the loft.

Abigail moved in her shaggy rug. She brought the old picture of the ship from the garage where Dad had left it and stuck it up on the dressing table. She spread a cloth on the floor for a picnic and laid out the plates from the loft. All the dolls and Hot Dog sat around waiting for something to eat so she tore up some paper from the drawing book to make cakes.

Mum came bouncing back in and the pieces of paper blew all over the room.

'You'll be able to keep this room really tidy,' she said. And then she tripped over Hot Dog, looked round and saw the muddle. It looked just like the loft before it had been tidied.

'I've made my own house,' said Abigail. 'And I'm going to keep it just like this for always.'

8 Abigail and the Thinner Dinner

Mum stopped on the way out to the shops one day and looked at herself in the hall mirror.

'I'm getting fat again,' she sighed.

'No you're not!' said Dad. He put his arms round her waist in a wide circle so that his fingers just touched in front.

'See,' he said. 'I can still cuddle you. Just about.'

'Very funny,' giggled Mum. She thumped him with her elbow. Abigail leaned against the door watching them.

'I think you're lovely,' she said.

'Thank you, Abigail,' said Mum, pulling on her coat. 'I think you're lovely too. But I'd be a lot lovelier if there wasn't so much of me. I'll start slimming again. We can have salad tonight.'

'Do we have to?' said Abigail. She didn't

like lettuce and tomatoes very much. 'Can't we have fish and chips again?'

'Too many chips make you fat,' said Mum. 'And lettuce is a thinner dinner.' She went off to find the shopping basket.

'*I'm* not fat,' said Abigail. She leaned against the hall table to look at herself in the mirror. She closed her mouth tight, and puffed out her

cheeks and tummy to see what she would look like if she was fat.

'Pudgy Pig!' laughed Dad. 'Come on, we'll miss the shops. Where's Paul?'

'Coming,' said Paul. He wandered through from the bedroom with his nose stuck in a book.

'Mum says . . .' said Abigail.

'I know, I heard,' said Paul, walking out to the car, still reading.

On the way to the shops, Abigail leaned over Mum's shoulder.

'Will I get fat when I'm grown up?' she asked.

'A rolling stone gathers no moss,' said Dad.

'What's that mean?' asked Abigail.

'It means,' said Mum, 'that you don't stand still long enough to get fat. Now sit back and be quiet.'

Abigail sat back and thought about that as they drove off through the traffic. She bounced forward again.

'*You* don't stand still,' she said.

'Sometimes do,' said Mum. 'Can't help it. It's the spaces in between rushing about, I suppose.'

The car slowed down at a crossing and stopped. There was a policeman on traffic duty. He was standing tall and straight in the middle of the road, waving cars and lorries

81

past. Abigail sat and watched him for what seemed a long time before he turned and waved to Dad.

'*He's* standing still,' she said. 'And he's not fat.'

'Just as well,' said Dad, starting up again. 'We'd never get round him if he was.' He pretended to pull on the steering wheel as if he was driving round a very large fat policeman, and Abigail giggled and bounced on the back seat.

'Sit still!' said Mum.

They turned the corner into the High Street, and Dad slowed down as a car moved out in front of them. In the back window there was a little white plastic skeleton. His long bony legs and feet jigged and danced as the car moved.

'Look,' said Abigail, pointing to the skeleton. 'He's been moving about a lot.'

'Aah,' said Dad. 'That's what happens to a Frightful Fidget who can't sit still for a minute. Make no bones about it.'

'Ooooooh,' said Paul and Mum together. 'That's awful.'

They parked the car behind the supermarket and collected a wire basket on the way in.

'Let's have a look at the vegetables,' said Mum. 'See what kind of a salad we could make.'

Paul and Abigail wandered along behind Mum and Dad. At the end of one of the display stands was a lady in a red and white dress. She was standing by a table decorated with red and white paper frills. Abigail stopped to look. The lady was tall and very thin, with lots of blue eye make-up and shiny silver ear-rings.

'*She's* standing . . .' Abigail whispered.

'Don't say it!' said Dad. The lady smiled and held out a plate full of little pieces of fruit loaf spread with butter.

'It's new,' she said. 'Would you like to try some?'

'Yes please,' said Dad, helping himself to a small piece. Abigail looked around the plate. She could see there was a bigger piece under-neath. She reached up and very carefully slid it out. Paul took a piece from the top and they all stood round, munching happily.

'Very good,' said Dad, and Paul and Abigail nodded.

Mum came back to see what they were doing.

'I thought we came to buy some salad,' she said, and then she saw the plate of fruit loaf.

'Would you like some?' asked the lady, smil-ing.

'My Mum's slimming,' said Abigail quickly. 'Can I have her bit?'

The lady laughed and held the plate out.

'Oh honestly!' said Mum, bouncing off to the vegetable counter, where the lettuce and tomatoes were spread out on a patch of plastic grass. Abigail stood beside her for a while stroking the grass. It felt soft and slippery, like fur.

'Can't decide about these tomatoes,' said Mum. 'What do you think?'

'Yuck!' said Abigail.

Mum and Dad took a long time choosing the salad. Paul had gone off to sit on the steps outside the shops with his book. Abigail wandered off round the shop to look at the shelves.

She stopped at the freezer cabinet where all the boxes of ice cream were, and, standing on tiptoe, leaned across the top. It made her face feel very cold.

She took a deep breath and puffed. Ha-roarrrrrrr! Her breath came out in a puff of smoke just like a dragon. She giggled and roared again. Ha-roarrrrrrrrr across the top of the pink cream boxes.

'I'm the Ice-Cream Dragon,' she growled to herself. She slid along the freezer cabinet and roared across the chocolate ice cream boxes.

It was when she was just coming down to the end of the cabinet, and roaring across the cream cakes, that she saw the VERY FAT MAN.

He was standing on the other side of the

freezer cabinet. Looking across, beneath the shelf with the cones and wafers, Abigail could only just see his middle in a grey knitted jersey.

It was the roundest, fattest middle she had ever seen!

She slid along to the end and peered round at his back. He was very wide, so wide that he almost blocked the whole of the space between the freezer and the next row of shelves. And he was just standing there, perfectly still, holding on to a basket and staring in front of him.

A little lady in a white straw hat came up, said something to him, and popped two tins in the basket. She went off again towards the meat counter.

Abigail slid back down the long side of the freezer again, up to the other end, to look at the man from the front.

He was not very tall. Not as tall as Dad, but he was very, very round.

His face was round and red with a little grey moustache that looked like a nail brush. He had two or three round wobbly chins, and when he took his cap off for a minute, Abigail could see that his head was round and shiny with no hair. His stomach in the grey knitted jersey was so round that his jacket stuck straight out at both sides.

Abigail stared at him. The Very Fat Man stared back and then looked away quickly, pretending he hadn't seen her. She stood watching to see if he would move. He stretched up and down on his toes once, and moved the basket to the other hand. But he still stood there, not moving. She slid closer. The Very Fat Man looked down at Abigail. He coughed. Harrrumph! His round grey jersey and all the chins wobbled like a jelly.

'It's considered rude to stare,' he said. 'Didn't do it when I was your size.'

He turned sideways on, but that blocked the space even more and a lady who was trying to get past had to lift her basket up and over his tummy.

Abigail stared at him. She couldn't imagine what he must have looked like when he was her size! She slid up beside him.

'I think you'd better move,' she said.

'Pardon?' said the Very Fat Man. He looked round. There was nobody trying to get past. 'Why do you say that?'

'My Dad says people get fat if they stand still too long,' said Abigail.

'Well really!' said the Very Fat Man.

'It'll be all right if you eat lettuce though,' she said quickly. 'My Mum says it's a thinner dinner.' The little lady in the straw hat, who had come back to put some sausages in the basket, laughed.

'Quite right too!' she said. 'What did I tell you, William?'

The Very Fat Man coughed again. His face had turned quite a different sort of red.

Just then Mum and Dad came up, looking for Abigail.

'Come on,' said Dad. 'We thought we'd lost you.' And then he saw the Very Fat Man's face.

'What's happened?' said Dad. 'What have you been up to?'

The Very Fat Man sniffed, turned and wobbled off without a word. The lady in the straw hat winked at Dad, smiled, and followed him humming a little tune to herself.

'What have you been doing?' asked Mum.

'Did you *see* him?' said Abigail. 'He was just standing there, getting fatter and FATTER!'

'Oh crikey!' said Mum and Dad together.

'But it's all right,' said Abigail. 'I told him about lettuce being a thinner dinner.'

Mum put her hands over her face and started to giggle.

'Honestly Abigail!' she said. 'I don't really think I want a salad tonight after all.'

'Great!' said Abigail. 'Does that mean we can have fish and chips after all?'

9 Abigail's Instant Giant Kit

Dad was working in the garage, sawing up pieces of wood to make something. Abigail was swinging backwards and forwards on the door, watching him.

'But why can't I go out on my trike?' she said. 'Paul goes down the road on his bike.'

Dad sighed and put down his saw.

'I've told you before,' he said. 'You're not big enough. When you're as big as Paul, then you can go out too. And don't swing on that, you'll pull the door down.'

Abigail sat down with a thump on an old box in the corner by the workbench.

'I'm fed up,' she said.

'What about?' said Dad. 'And please don't sit on my tube of glue or you'll be stuck up too.'

'Paul's BIGGER than me,' said Abigail.

'Well he can't help that,' said Dad. 'He's

older than you too, so he's bound to be bigger.'

'But he's ALWAYS bigger than me,' said Abigail. 'It's not fair. I want to grow quicker.' She scuffed her feet about in the sawdust on the garage floor.

Dad stopped what he was doing and thought about it for a moment.

'Tell you what,' he said. 'Leave it with me. 'I'll see what I can do about it.' He rummaged about among some pieces of wood at the back of the garage.

'What are you going to do?' asked Abigail, jumping up. 'Can I help? Can you make me bigger than Paul?'

'Just wait and see,' said Dad. He shooed Abigail out of the garage and refused to say any more. Even when he came out for a tea-break and Abigail offered him half of her chocolate biscuit, he smiled but still said nothing at all.

All through lunch Abigail kept asking:

'What is it?' and 'What are you making?' until everyone was thoroughly fed-up listening to her, and Mum said she could finish her lunch in the kitchen on her own if she didn't stop talking. But still Dad said nothing. He finished his cup of tea, very slowly, and then went back out to the garage.

Half-an-hour later he called to everyone to come out and see what he had made.

He had two long thin strips of wood, a little taller than Abigail, and rounded at the top, like handles. Part of the way up each one, just about level with Abigail's knees, he had fixed on a block of wood.

'Is that it?' said Abigail, a little bit disappointed.

'That's it,' said Dad.

'But what is it?' said Abigail.

'Guess,' said Dad.

'They're for getting the football down off the garage roof,' said Paul.

'No,' said Dad. 'But it's a good idea.'

'They're for poking out all that rubbish underneath Abigail's bed,' said Mum.

'Nope!' said Dad again. 'But that's a VERY good idea. They are, actually ... an Instant Giant Kit!'

'Instant Giant Kit!' said Abigail, Mum and Paul all at once.

'S'right,'' said Dad. 'They're called stilts. If you hold on to the handle and stand up on the blocks it makes you much taller. Bigger even than Paul. Then you can try and walk around like that too. Go on, have a shot.'

Abgail put one foot up on a block, held on tight to the handles and tried to step up on to the other stilt with her other foot. The stilts wobbled a bit and she jumped down again.

'Lean against the wall,' said Mum. 'It's easier to get on that way.'

Abigail stood with her back against the garage wall and climbed up on to both stilts. She stood up straight and held on very tightly.

'I'm bigger than Paul,' she shouted. 'I'm nearly as big as Mummy!'

Then, still holding on very tightly, she took one wobbly step forward, then another and a third before she had to jump off again.

'You've got it,' said Dad. 'Keep trying.' He went back into the garage to get on with his work.

'Can I have a shot?' asked Paul.

'No!' said Abigail. 'They're mine. And if you stand on them you'd be even MORE bigger than me.'

'Stupid things anyway,' said Paul. 'You can't play football with them.' He ran off down to the park to look for his friends.

Abigail went up and down the path until she could walk really well on the stilts. They made a lovely clunk, clunk, clunk sound on the path. She walked all round the little pond, and then, because no-one was looking, she walked right through the middle, without getting her sandals even a little bit wet. She was just turning round to do it again when Dad poked his head out of the garage.

'Don't let your Mum catch you at that!' he said. 'Or we'll both be in trouble.'

Abigail clunked off up the path leaving funny little square wet footprints. She went round to the living room window at the front of the house. Usually she couldn't see in because the window sill was too high but today it was different. She pressed her nose flat against the glass.

'Hello,' said Mum from inside. 'That's a shocking horrible face looking in my window.'

'I'm a giant that eats people,' said Abigail, and she stuck out her tongue and made a really dreadful face.

'I can well believe it!' said Mum. 'And kindly don't dribble on my clean windows.'

Abigail giggled and went off to be a giant somewhere else. Clunk, clunk, clunk across to the lawn. There was a flower bed along the edge of the grass and Abigail took one giant step, right over it, flowers and all, on to the grass under the little beech tree.

On the stilts, her head was up in among the lower branches of the tree and she was just level with the coconut shell that the blue tits swung on. She poked it with her nose till it swung backwards and forwards. Then back she went across the flower bed with another huge step.

Clunk, clunk, clunk, she stepped out on to the pavement, and along to old Mr. Campbell's garden next door. Mr. Campbell was a friend of Abigail's and she very often stopped to talk to him. He was quite a lot older than Abigail's Dad, and he spent a lot of time working in his garden.

Abigail stood beside his hedge. Most days it was a high hedge that came to just above her head, but today was different. Today she was bigger than the hedge, and she could see right over to the other side, where Mr. Campbell,

in his old waistcoat and brown cap, was weeding the rose bed.

'Hello,' shouted Abigal.

'Who said that?' said Mr. Campbell looking up, very surprised.

'Me,' said Abigail. 'I can see right over your hedge today.'

'My word, so you can,' said Mr. Campbell. He took his glasses out of the little tin case in his waistcoat pocket, put them on the end of his nose, and peered at her through them.

'It's Abigail!' he said. 'I can't imagine what your mother feeds you on. I've never known a child grow so fast.'

Abigail laughed so much she nearly fell off her stilts.

'My Dad made me an Instant Giant Kit,' she said. 'I'm bigger than Paul now – even if he IS older than me.'

Mr. Campbell came up to the hedge and looked over at the stilts.

'Well I never,' he said. 'Clever man, your Dad. And do you know, I do believe you're bigger than me too, and I'M older than Paul. I'm even older than your Dad. In fact I'm probably the oldest person in the road. But you're actually BIGGER than me.'

'So I am!' said Abigail, looking down on the top of old Mr. Campbell's brown gardening cap. 'So I must be the biggest person in the whole street!'

And she clunked off down the road to tell everyone about it.